Sarah

AND THE

NAKED TRUTH

Also by Elisa Carbone

Starting School with an Enemy

Stealing Freedom

Sarah
AND THE
NAKED TRUTH

BY ELISA CARBONE

ALFRED A. KNOPF, NEW YORK

THIS IS A BORZOI BOOK PUBLISHED BY ALFRED A. KNOPF

Copyright © 2000 by Elisa Carbone
Jacket and text illustrations copyright © 2000 by Tim Barnes

www.randomhouse.com/kids

Library of Congress Cataloging-in-Publication Data
Carbone, Elisa Lynn.
Sarah and the naked truth / by Elisa Carbone.
p. cm.
Summary: While ten-year-old Sarah faces some challenges after losing most
of her hair in a bubble gum accident, her closest friends Christina and Olivia
deal with identity issues of their own, and in the end all learn to
stand up to others in order to be true to themselves.

ISBN 0-375-80264-9 (trade). — ISBN 0-375-90264-3 (lib. bdg.)
[1. Best friends—Fiction. 2. Friendship—Fiction.] I. Title.
PZ7.C1865Sar   2000
[Fic]—dc21   99-33714

Printed in the United States of America

April 2000

10 9 8 7 6 5 4 3 2 1

KNOPF, BORZOI BOOKS, and the colophon are
registered trademarks of Random House, Inc.

To Mom and Dad,
with love

With special thanks to Alice,
who let her stories become part of this story

Sarah
AND THE
NAKED
TRUTH

ONE

One look in my bedroom mirror let me know I was in big trouble.

In the hall I passed my older brother, Jerod, who was mostly asleep and on his way to the bathroom. The sight of me must have shocked him awake, because he opened his eyes real wide and cried, "W'appen tuyr *hair?*"

I didn't answer but marched down the steps, where I almost collided with my dad, who was on his way up with his bare belly hanging over a pair of paisley boxer shorts and his hair stuffed into a shower cap. His mouth dropped open, but he didn't say anything. If he had, I think I still could have proven that he looked funnier than me.

In the kitchen, my mom was standing at the counter dressed in a suit, sipping coffee from a mug, which she almost dropped when she saw me. It must have looked like a pink alien was trying to suck me into a black hole, starting with my head.

If you want to know when the whole problem started, I guess you'd have to go all the way back to Halloween. That's when my best friend, Christina, and I went trick-or-treating dressed as werewolves. We had plastic fangs and wigs of electric green fur. And we each stuck some of those fake blood pellets in our mouths, bit into them, and let the slimy red stuff ooze down our chins. It tasted pretty bad, but it was worth it for the effect. We got a ton of candy and even managed to avoid Eric Bardo and his friends Roger and Lawrence. We saw them throw an egg at Mr. Cohen's house (which, of course, we mentioned to Mr. Cohen when we knocked on his door and it was dripping with egg), and we heard from some other kids that they were grabbing little kids' bags of

2

candy and throwing them around. Those guys are like the neighborhood pimples: you know they're there, but you wish they weren't. Not that I'd know anything about pimples yet, because I'm still just ten, but I learned about them from my brother Jerod, who's fifteen and knows about these things. Anyhow, Christina and I were really glad we didn't have any run-ins with those three, and we got back to my house with our bags of candy intact.

As it turns out, Christina doesn't like bubble gum. Don't ask me why, because I never asked her, I just traded all my lollipops and caramels for all of her bubble gum. I love bubble gum. Or at least I did then, before it started causing weird things to happen to me.

I guess it wasn't the bubble gum itself that caused the weird stuff. It was what I did with it. I should have left it in my underwear drawer. I put it in there so my parents wouldn't say, "That's too much bubble gum, Sarah Marie. It's going to rot your teeth.

Throw it away." If I'd left it under my Fruit of the Looms, it wouldn't have been a problem. And if I'd chewed it one piece at a time, or two or three, and in broad daylight, then it wouldn't have been a big deal, either. But I didn't.

First, I forgot all about it for a few months. I did wonder every once in a while why my underwear smelled like bubble gum, but I didn't think that much about it. I was too busy getting ready for the Thanksgiving play Mr. Harrison had our class put on, in which I played a Native American and got to braid my hair and spray-paint it black. Then there was Christmastime, which is when Jerod told Aunt Connie that he wished people would give him cash for Christmas instead of presents he didn't like, so she gave him one of those little-kid piggy banks with a bunch of pennies in it, just to teach him to be more polite.

During January and February, it never snowed once, and I realized that these people here in Maryland don't even know what real winter *looks* like. It wasn't until early March that the bubble gum surfaced again. It was nighttime and I was in my p.j.'s, ready to go to bed. I started rummaging around in all of my drawers for something green to wear on St. Patrick's Day so I wouldn't get smacked at school. That's when I found the stash of bubble gum. I was so excited, I unwrapped a piece and chewed it right then and there. It tasted great, so I added about four more until I had a nice fat wad in my mouth. It was delicious. I blew a bubble the size of a cantaloupe and decided this wad of gum was too good to waste. I went to bed still chewing it, and as I was falling asleep, I stuck it in the side of my cheek for safe-keeping.

That was how I discovered that a cheek is *not* a good place to store chewed-up bubble gum. When I woke up in the morning, none of the gum was in my mouth and all of it was in my hair.

I recognized right away that this was the kind of situation you can't hide from your parents, so that's when I marched downstairs to ask Mom what I should do.

"Oh, Sarah," Mom said, partly mad and partly really disappointed because she knew what I was about to find out: I was going to lose most of my hair.

Bubble gum, it turns out, doesn't wash out, wear out, pull out, cook out, or even freeze out of hair. It stays *with* the hair. So if you want to get rid of the gum, you have to get rid of the hair.

My mom called her boss to say she had a family emergency and would be a little late for work. In our house, my mom is the one who wears suits and goes to an office, and my dad is the one with the long hair. That's because my mom's new job with the government is the whole reason we left Maine and moved to Maryland in the first place, and my dad does carpentry work, and his customers don't care about his hair just as long as he makes their kitchens and bathrooms look good.

Mom sat me down and took out a very mean-looking pair of scissors. I closed my eyes and felt her pulling on the gum and snipping hair. After a lot of snipping, she finally said, "I think I got it all out."

I peeked in a mirror and saw that one side of my head had your basic "recently mowed" look: hair about an inch long prickling out. It only seemed reasonable to cut the rest of my hair to match. That's when I started wearing a baseball cap to school.

That was also about the time Olivia moved in. When I first moved here last August, I didn't think there were any girls my age in the neighborhood because Christina hadn't come back yet from visiting her relatives in El Salvador. So when the moving truck arrived at the town houses down the road, and it turned out we were going to have *three* girls in Mr. Harrison's fifth-grade class all in the same neighborhood, I was really happy.

I remembered how nervous I'd been about starting school in a new place, so I made myself into a regular welcoming committee for Olivia. She wasn't just moving from another state, either. She'd come all the way from Trinidad. She was tall like me and had long black hair that was frizzy and soft. She had a nice accent that made her sound like she was reciting poetry whenever she talked, and her skin was almost as dark brown as Mr. Harrison's.

I liked Olivia right from the start. The day after she moved in, I invited her over. I took her up to my room to show her my Boston Celtics banner, my baby seal poster, and the pictures of me and Christina making silly faces in the photo booth at the mall. She laughed at the pictures of me and Christina and said she really liked the Boston Celtics, which I thought was very impressive for someone from Trinidad. My closet was partway open, and at one point Olivia peeked inside with this worried look on her face, like maybe there was an ax murderer hiding in there. I closed it for her and decided it was time to go over to Christina's.

At Christina's, we went up to her room and let her

hamster, Tito, run around on her bed for a while. When Olivia peered into Christina's closet with that same worried look, I was beginning to think she was a bit paranoid.

But then she said, "Could I have a peek at your school uniform? My mother hasn't bought mine yet, and I want to see how horrid it looks."

Christina and I stared at each other for a second, then Christina laughed and said, "I see, they must wear school uniforms in Trinidad like some of my cousins in El Salvador do, and boy are they ugly—all old-fashioned and boring colors—well, at our school you wear whatever you want, jeans or sweatpants or anything except sunglasses—Mr. Harrison doesn't let us wear sunglasses in class, or beepers, either."

Christina talks like that sometimes, with everything coming out in one burst that you have to listen to real fast if you want to keep up with her.

Olivia grinned. "I think I'll like this school," she said.

That's when Tito pooped on Christina's bedspread and we had to put him back in his cage, but we were off to a great start with Olivia.

The first day Olivia came to school, Christina and I begged and whined until Mr. Harrison put her into our cooperative learning group. We had just lost Kelly because she switched to another school, and we knew Jamal wanted a boy to be added to our group instead, but we told Jamal he was just going to be stuck with three girls for the rest of the year. He made a disgusted face, but I don't think he really minded. Christina and I are a couple of the best soccer players in the class, and we're always on Jamal's team during recess. Sometimes we start talking about game strategies in class when we're done with our work. In our cooperative learning groups, we sit facing each other with our desks pushed together, so it makes it easy to talk.

That first day, just before lunch, and even before

we'd finished our Language Arts work sheets, we started discussing soccer.

"I figured out what Tyrone's weak point is," said Christina. "If you kick a goal in high, he almost never stops it. I think he's afraid of getting hit in the head."

Jamal nodded.

"Olivia, you want to play soccer during recess?" I asked. "We get a great game going almost every day."

Olivia grinned. "Sure. That sounds fun," she said.

But then, if you've ever seen a baking cake pouffe up nice and high and then smush right down flat when you slam the oven door, you know exactly what Olivia's face did. One minute, she was smiling real big, saying she wanted to play soccer, and the next minute, she looked like a flat, unhappy cake.

"Actually, no," she said. "I don't want to play."

That was the beginning of the mystery about Olivia.

TWO

"How's this?" Olivia gave me a shy smile and handed me the notepad she'd been scribbling on all during our soccer game.

I took one look and my mouth dropped open. There we were, drawn in pencil and colored in with Magic Marker: Christina with her skinny brown legs and black curly hair, me with what was left of my blond hair sticking out from under my black-and-orange Orioles baseball cap, and Jamal with his ripped-in-the-knee jeans and his short dreadlocks. But it wasn't just us playing soccer, colored in with all the right colors. It actually looked like us. I mean, she'd gotten the way Christina's round eyes kind of light up and sparkle, and the way Jamal's square chin and down-turned mouth make him look so serious most of the time.

By now, Christina and some of the other kids were admiring the picture, too.

"How did you learn to do that?" asked Christina.

Olivia shrugged. "I just *know* how, that's all."

"Can you teach other people how to do it?" I asked. I was thinking how great it would be to draw a picture of Eric, Roger, and Lawrence in just their underwear and pass it around the school.

"I could try," she offered.

During the afternoon, Christina and Jamal went to Social Studies with the other fifth-grade teacher, Mrs. Green, and Olivia and I stayed with Mr. Harrison's group. We had to read a chapter in our Social Studies book about the gods of ancient Greece and then write down the answers to a bunch of questions. When I was almost done answering my questions, I looked over at Olivia. She had finished writing, and she was drawing Zeus.

"How do you do that?" I whispered.

"Here." She showed me the picture of Zeus in the book. "First you look at where the light parts and the dark parts are."

I could see that one half of his face was darker than the other, like it was in the shade.

"Then you look at the shapes," she whispered.

Zeus' face was shaped like an upside-down pear. I started drawing. But when I finished, it did not look like Zeus, the mighty king of all the gods. It looked more like one of the seven dwarfs on a bad day.

I groaned. "I think I'm going to need more lessons," I said.

Olivia nodded as she examined my handiwork. "A lot more," she said.

Christina and I walked Olivia home after school. I've noticed that on some days you can ask a person lots of questions and they seem happy to answer them, and on other days when you ask even a few questions, they just get mad. I think that day was a bad question day for Olivia.

"Do you miss your old town?" asked Christina.

Olivia sighed and looked a little sad. "Yeah," she said.

"My grandmother and cousins and everybody still live in El Salvador," said Christina. "I only see them in the summer, and I miss them a lot. Did you leave any relatives back in Trinidad?"

"We left my *father* there!" Olivia said. "I *really* miss him. And everyone else, too."

Christina and I were both surprised.

"Why didn't your dad come with you?" I asked.

"He had to work," she said.

"Is he going to come here soon?" I asked.

Olivia shook her head and frowned.

"Are your parents getting a divorce?" I asked.

"No!" she said loudly, and gave me a very annoyed look.

The three of us walked without saying anything for a minute. Then Christina asked, "Did you come here to see relatives?"

"No," Olivia said. She still seemed upset.

Christina rolled her eyes. "So why did you come?"

Olivia stopped walking and crossed her arms over her chest. "We just *came,* all right?"

I figured it was a great time to change the subject. "Isn't it ever going to snow here?" I blurted out. Olivia started walking again. "In Maine, we'd have had tons of snow by now," I said.

Christina looked up at the sky. It was gray with winter clouds. "Some years it snows, some years it doesn't," she said.

"I hope it snows this year," said Olivia. "I'd like to see it just once."

That's when *I* stopped walking. "You've never seen snow?!"

Olivia raised her shoulders and held out her

16

hands, palms up. "Where am I going to find snow in Trinidad? I've seen it on the television, but I've never touched it."

Christina pumped her fist in the air. "Great. The first time it snows, we'll all three meet at my house for a snowball fight."

"What if it's on a school day?" I asked.

Christina looked at me cross-eyed. "They'll close school, silly."

Every once in a while, I still ask a dumb question because things were so different in Maine. Up there, they don't close school every time it snows—only for really big snows. I decided to change the subject again.

"Anyone want to come try out for a basketball team with me?" I'd seen the card on a bulletin board at the grocery store. It said this church team needed new players, ages 9, 10, and 11. With my parents both working, I knew I'd have to ride my bike to the church and back in the cold. I had this idea that maybe Olivia would want to try out and maybe her mom could drive us. "Tryouts are this afternoon," I said hopefully.

"No," said Olivia.

"No, thanks," said Christina.

I pouted at them. "You mean I have to go by myself?"

"You're the one who loves basketball," said Christina.

She was right. I'm the one who learned to dribble a Spalding almost before I was potty-trained and who can sometimes beat my big brother Jerod in Horse. And I was the one who came up with the brilliant idea that it would be fun to ride my bike through all kinds of weather twice a week to a church three miles away from my house so I could get yelled at by some coach.

"I'd better get going so I can start pedaling," I said.

I left them standing on Olivia's doorstep and trotted home. When I stopped by my house to get my bike, I found Jerod sitting at the kitchen table reading his mail.

"Yo, Sarah, wassup?" he said.

"Wassup?" I said.

He was staring at what looked like a Hallmark card, and he seemed confused.

"What's that?" I asked.

"Invitation."

"To what?"

"Party."

"What kind?"

"Birthday."

"Whose?"

He looked up at me with a sly little grin. "Sheila's."

"Good deal!" I said. I knew enough from hearing him talk with his friends that he had a crush on this girl Sheila.

He went back to staring at the card like it was going to bite him.

"So what's the problem?" I asked. Jerod seemed to be having a good question day.

"It says, 'Come as you are.'"

"What's that supposed to mean?"

He threw the card on the table and sighed. "That's the problem. I have no idea what it means."

"Ask Mom," I said. I didn't want to be late for the basketball tryouts, so I grabbed a banana and headed to the garage for my bike.

Our neighborhood is pretty hilly, and I don't know which was worse: pumping my bike up the hills until I got sweaty, or zooming down the hills in the icy wind until the sweat froze right on my skin. By the time I got to the church, my fingers and ears felt like Popsicles.

I parked my bike and found the door marked BASKETBALL TEAM TRYOUTS HERE. Inside, it was nice and warm, and I followed the sound of bouncing basketballs to a huge gym in the school part of the church. There were a few parents sitting in chairs along the sides, and a lot of kids my age messing around on the court. A tall white guy with graying hair came up to me. I figured he must be the coach.

"You here to try out?" he asked. He didn't smile, just looked me up and down like he was trying to figure out if I was coordinated or not.

"Yeah," I said.

"Your mom or dad here?"

"No."

He shoved a clipboard under my nose. "Write your name here." He pointed to the last line under a list of names and handed me a pen.

There was space for last name, first name, and middle initial. I wrote *Gajeski.* Then, just as I was writing *Sarah*, I got hit in the elbow with a bouncing basketball. The pen scribbled, and it looked like I'd written *Sableeeh* or something. I printed my middle initial, *M* for Marie, but before I could fix my first name, the coach snatched the clipboard away and went to talk to another kid who'd just walked in.

The boy who'd hit me with the ball bounced it at

me again, and this time I caught it. Then he came after me to try to steal it, and I spun around, dribbled away, darted in between the other kids, and swished a hook shot.

The boy grinned at me. "Good shot," he said. "I hope you make the team." He had a shock of blond hair on the top of his head, and the sides of his head were shaved. He looked a little older than me, so I figured he was one of the eleven-year-olds.

The coach called everyone over to sit down. He explained how the team had had a couple of kids move away, one kid break a leg, and another one get mono, and they needed new players so they could finish the season. He said we'd line up and each shoot nine times, three from the right, three from the left, and three from the foul line. The four kids who got the most baskets would make the team. I thought that was a dumb way to do it, since he wouldn't find out anything about how well we could shoot during a game, but I didn't mind because I got the most in of everybody: seven out of nine.

The coach got the phone numbers and addresses of the kids who'd made the team and sent everyone else home. The blond kid came up to me with his hands in his pockets. "Glad you got on," he said. "I saw the list—okay if I just call you Sam? No way I can pronounce your name."

I laughed. "That's because you bumped me while I was writing!" I thought Sam was a pretty cool nickname, though, so I said he could call me that. He told me his name was Doug and he was the team captain. For the next half-hour he took turns playing one-on-one with me and this other kid, Luther, who was also new. Doug said me and Luther were better than any of the kids they'd lost, and he thought maybe now the team had a chance to start winning some games.

I decided to ride my bike home before my parents got worried and before it got pitch-dark outside.

Back in Maine, it would have been dark about an hour ago. And in Maine, if I'd ridden my bike to a church three miles from my house, I would have probably known half the kids there. But here in Silver Spring, Maryland, where there are apartment buildings and town houses and about a zillion people and a hundred different schools, I didn't recognize a single person in the whole gym. I have to admit, Maryland still takes some getting used to.

THREE

At dinner, I told Mom and Dad and Jerod about making the team. Jerod said, "Wayduhgo, Sarah!" but Mom and Dad looked unhappy, even though they were saying things like "That's great."

"Are the games only on Saturdays, sweetie?" Mom asked. "Are you sure there are no evening games, or maybe Sundays?"

I was about to explain to her that it was a church team, so they couldn't very well play on Sunday, when I figured out why she looked so sorry. She was going to be taking a computer class all day on Saturdays for the next few months.

"And practices are Wednesday *afternoons* only?"

Dad was asking me. "No evenings, either?" He works Saturdays a lot, too.

"Look, you guys," I said. "I didn't join this basketball team to make you feel guilty. I did it to have fun, which I can do even if you never make it to a game or a practice, okay?"

They both looked relieved. There are times when I *try* to make my parents feel guilty, but this wasn't one of them.

After that, I told them how I messed up writing my name, so the team captain nicknamed me Sam. They laughed, and Jerod offered to play one-on-one with me whenever I wanted to practice. Before I went to bed, I called first Christina and then Olivia to tell them I'd made the team, and they were both really happy for me.

At school the next day, Olivia was absent. Christina and I offered to bring her the schoolwork she'd missed, so Mr. Harrison gave us her assignment sheets.

"And if she's really sick, we can bring stuff to her every day until she gets better," said Christina as we walked to Olivia's house.

I nodded. "Don't you wonder why she moved here?" I asked.

"Yeah, but I don't think she's going to tell us," said Christina.

"Or why she was all excited about soccer when we first asked her, but now she'll never play?"

Christina shrugged. "Maybe she just likes to draw. She never plays anything during recess. She just draws."

I was beginning to think maybe I was making too much of a big deal about the mysterious things Olivia had done. But then we got to her town house, and the mystery got even bigger.

Olivia's mom, Mrs. Mooloo, opened the door. She was tall and slender and dark, with thin fingers and graceful hands. "Hello, Sarah, hello, Christina. How nice of you to come by," she said. Her accent was just as much like poetry as Olivia's.

"We brought Olivia's schoolwork," said Christina. "We're sorry she's sick."

"Oh, no, she is not sick. Not sick at all," said Mrs. Mooloo.

Olivia appeared from around the corner and smiled at us.

"Lili, your friends are here to see you. You have plenty of time to visit before supper," said her mother.

Olivia took us up to her room. Her drawings were hung all over her walls, and she had a card table that was covered with sheets of drawing paper, pens, Magic Markers, and things called Cray-Pas, which looked like a cross between chalk and crayons. She held up a large drawing of a girl in a baseball cap holding a basketball. I stared at it a second, then realized it was *me!*

"This is to say congratulations on making the

team," said Olivia, and she handed me the drawing.

"Wow, thanks," I said, but my mind was still on the subject of how a kid can get away with missing school when she's not sick.

Christina was drawing on her hand with a red Cray-Pas. "Look, I'm bleeding!" she cried.

"You want to try those?" asked Olivia. "They smear really well, so you can make a picture look soft if you want it to." She pulled out three clean sheets of drawing paper.

"Olivia, how come you weren't in school today?" I asked. But as soon as I said it, I was sorry.

Olivia swung around to face me and narrowed her eyes. "Sarah, why do you have to know everything?"

I didn't answer her question, and she didn't answer mine.

Christina said, "Come on, you guys, let's just draw, okay?"

After that, I sat around feeling stupid that I'd

asked Olivia another bad question, while Olivia showed Christina how to smear Cray-Pas all over the place. It wouldn't have done me any good to try to draw, anyway, since I'm no good at it.

The next day at school, we had what my parents like to call an "educational experience." Christina got up during Language Arts to get a dictionary from the back of the room. All of a sudden, we heard her yelp. When we looked up, she was staring at our science experiment.

We have these science experiments that each cooperative learning group started at the beginning of the year. At first, they seemed interesting: each group got a bunch of squirmy white larvae to put in a glass terrarium along with stuff we gathered from the woods outside—pine cones, rotting tree bark, and anything else we thought larvae might like. The larvae were supposed to decide which junk they liked best—ours picked the tree bark—and live there until they changed into pupae, and then into adult insects. At first, we could hardly wait for them to change, and we checked every day to see if they'd turned into butterflies or something. Our group had to get some new larvae in the middle of the experiment, but that's another story. Anyway, after a while it got pretty boring because they just stayed looking like chopped-up spaghetti. We forgot about them.

So when Christina yelped, we thought maybe we finally had butterflies. Jamal, Olivia, and I rushed to our terrarium, and some of the other kids went over to look at theirs. That's when I got really mad.

"Mr. Harrison, a bunch of beetles got into our science experiment and ate all our larvae!" I shouted.

Mr. Harrison came over to see.

"That's not fair," said Jamal.

"We should have put the top on tighter," said Christina.

All that waiting for nothing. I pouted at the shiny

copper-and-green beetles crawling all around our terrarium.

Mr. Harrison put one hand on my shoulder and another on Jamal's. "What do you think *actually* happened?" he asked.

At that minute, I was thinking that what had *actually* happened was that some mean sixth graders had decided it would be funny to wreck our science experiment. Or that maybe the strongest beetle had held the terrarium top open so all the other beetles could crawl in, saying, "Get your delicious juicy larvae, right here!"

"I think what actually happened is that we didn't put the top on tight enough," said Christina.

Olivia was peering into the terrarium. "I think you got beetles instead of butterflies," she said simply.

Christina, Jamal, and I all dropped our mouths open. I guess that's what you call an educational experience.

It turned out we weren't allowed to set the beetles free because they were Japanese beetles and they like to eat people's roses. But we were allowed to bring in vegetables for them. I guess that way they'd only eat what they had permission to.

We were also allowed to put them in a jar with a cotton ball soaked in alcohol to kill them and then stab them through with long needles to mount them in a box with a label on it. Mr. Harrison said that would be part of learning about Entomology. Our group thought that sounded more like Cruelty to Insects and decided to keep them as pets. We set up a feeding schedule, with one of us bringing in celery leaves or potato peels every day.

That afternoon, Christina and Jamal came back from Social Studies with Mrs. Green's group and said they were going to put on a "cultural pageant" after spring break. Christina was all excited about it. "Everybody will get to represent the state or country their family is from," she said. "That means I'll get to go onstage and talk about El Salvador."

Olivia and I said it sounded really fun and that we wished Mr. Harrison's group would get to do something like that.

On Friday, Olivia missed school again, and when Christina and I brought her work over, she wasn't sick. I didn't ask anything this time, though. And I did let her show me how to use the Cray-Pas, which I smeared to make a picture of the earth being formed during the Big Bang. No one else could tell that was what it was a picture of, but *I* knew, and Olivia said that was the important thing.

FOUR

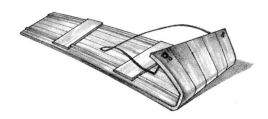

When I woke up Sunday morning, there was this weird, eerie quiet in my room. At first I thought maybe I had water in my ears. Then I remembered what makes that kind of quiet, and when I threw open my shades, I found out I was right. It had *snowed!* There were at least four inches on the ground, and it was still falling.

"Yippee!" I yelled. My mom peeked in my door and shushed me because Dad was still sleeping.

"I'm going out in the snow with Christina and Olivia, okay?" I said more softly.

"That's fine," she said. "Does Olivia have everything she needs?"

"I could bring an extra toboggan," I suggested.

"You'd better call and see if she has boots and snow pants, too," said Mom.

I thought Mom was being silly. How can anyone get through childhood without boots and snow pants? But just to be polite, I called Olivia.

"It's so lovely!" Olivia yelled into the phone. "And *cold,* and it tastes . . . well, it froze my tongue. I love it!"

She was so excited, I thought she might wake my dad up right through the phone.

It turned out she did not have boots and had never even heard of snow pants. In fact, she'd gone outside in her slippers and pajamas—that's how much she knew about what you're supposed to wear in the snow!

"Do you have waterproof mittens?" I asked. "Those blue wool ones you wear to school will get wet in no time."

She needed snow mittens, too. It turns out nobody needs any of those things in Trinidad. It's a good thing I'm from Maine, because I had extras of everything. And it was a good thing I had the toboggans, too, because by the time I hung up the phone with Olivia, I was bringing the entire kids' clothing section of Sears over to her house, so I dragged everything over on the toboggans. Before I left, I called Christina and told her to meet me at Olivia's.

Olivia thought the snow pants were really funny. "It's like a duvet for my bum!" she said, giggling.

Then, when Christina and I didn't know what a duvet was (turns out it's a fluffy bed quilt), she thought that was even funnier. We were all laughing, getting Olivia bundled up, and she said she was feeling more and more like a mummy, when we got to the boots. That's when, apparently, I asked another bad question.

"You've got to take your sneakers off first," I said. "You want me to help you stuff your feet in?"

Olivia looked suddenly shocked.

"I don't have any foot diseases or anything," I said. "Is that what you're worried about?"

"I'm not worried about *anything*," she snapped, and marched upstairs carrying the boots.

"*Now* what did I say wrong?" I threw up my hands and widened my eyes at Christina. She was redoing the Velcro on her own boots.

"She probably was tired of us dressing her like she was a doll or something, and she maybe has to pee before we go outside, and she wants to leave her shoes in her bedroom instead of scattered around here in the hallway, and maybe she even wants to look in the mirror and see how she looks in all the new clothes," Christina suggested.

Mrs. Mooloo came to check on us. "How are you girls doing?"

"Olivia's just getting her boots on," I said.

"Good, good. She's very excited about the snow, you know. With spring just around the corner, we thought we'd missed our chance to see it." She put on her coat and gloves and said she'd walk to the store while we were out, but that there was plenty of cheese and cucumbers for sandwiches if we wanted lunch before she got back. Olivia had already told us how cheese-and-cucumber sandwiches are a typical lunch in Trinidad, and I thought it would be interesting to try one.

Olivia came down the steps with the boots on.

"They fit okay?" I asked.

She nodded.

I was getting awfully sweaty in all my layers. Instead of my baseball cap I was wearing my wool hat, and with no hair to cover my ears, the wool was making them itch. I was really glad when we finally stepped outside.

Olivia immediately took off her mittens, picked up a big handful of snow from the ground, and started eating it.

"Your hands are going to get cold," I said.

She nodded enthusiastically. "Isn't it amazing

how it does that?" She chomped into the snow with her teeth. "It makes your mouth very cold, too."

"Let's let Olivia pick what she wants to do," said Christina. "Sledding, snowball fight, snow angels, or snowman building."

"I want to do *everything*," said Olivia.

We started by lying down to make snow angels, because the front yard was perfect for them. And since Olivia's yard was so tiny, with room for only two angels, we gave angels to all the other town houses on her row, too. Olivia's hands turned red with the cold, and she finally put the mittens back on. Then we pulled our toboggans up to the school to get some sledding in before the rest of the neighborhood kids wore all the snow off the hill.

"You steer it by leaning," Christina explained. "And you just have to watch out for the sewer drain at the bottom."

The sewer drain was made of concrete, like a big

slab of sidewalk that had ended up in a field instead of along a road. It had a metal rim, sat up about eight inches above the ground, and basically looked like something you could kill yourself on. Christina said a kid hit it headfirst last year and had to go to the hospital for stitches. I dragged our toboggans over to the left, as far from the drain as we could get.

There were already a couple of little kids sledding, but they hadn't wrecked the snow yet. Our first time down, we crammed all three of us onto one toboggan, with Olivia in the middle so she could get the hang of it while Christina and I steered. Olivia screeched all the way and looked a little shaken up when we got out at the bottom, but she said she liked it. On our way back up the hill, she slipped and fell, so I fell, too, just to make her feel more at home.

At the top, Olivia surprised us by announcing, "I'm ready to try it by myself." She screeched all the way down again, and I finally figured out that it was happy screeching rather than get-me-out-of-here screeching. Christina and I started screeching on our rides, too, and it was so much fun, we did it louder each time. Then the little kids started squealing and yelling until it sounded like we were all being attacked by Godzilla. The lady from the house closest to the sledding hill came out in a jacket, boots, and a nightgown to tell us to be quiet.

Just our luck, when we turned around from being yelled at by the lady in the nightgown, we found ourselves being laughed at by Eric and Roger, two of the neighborhood pimples. They were both carrying big silver saucer sleds.

"Hey, wacko Sarah. You're in trouble again, I see," Eric shouted.

I felt like saying, "Who let you out of your cage?" but I managed to keep my mouth shut so that maybe we could keep on sledding without too much hassle from them.

"Leave her alone, Bardo," said Roger. "Can't you see she's too embarrassed to talk about it?"

They both cracked up and set their saucers right where we'd been going down.

"Hey, shove over," I said. "This is our spot."

"Not anymore," said Eric.

"Let's just move," said Christina quietly.

We tried to ignore them and steer clear of them, but it seemed like every time I went down the hill, one of those guys was right there next to me, pushing me farther and farther over, until one time I almost hit the sewer drain. That's when I figured out what they were doing.

I went running up the hill to warn Olivia, who was just starting down. Roger ran toward her with his saucer and plopped down, heading straight at her. She steered right to avoid him, looking back at him instead of ahead.

"Olivia! The sewer drain!" I yelled. "Watch out!"

It was too late. Olivia was speeding out of control,

straight for the drain. She crashed into it, left leg first, and Roger crashed into her. Olivia's leg got jammed between her sled and the concrete.

Christina and I raced down the hill. Olivia held her leg, crying, "Oh no, oh no!"

Roger got to his feet and just stood there dumbfounded, like he hadn't figured out that if you steer someone into a slab of concrete at high speed, it could hurt them.

"Pull up your pant leg. You might need stitches," said Christina.

"*Noooo!*" Olivia wailed. "My mother will kill me!"

"No, she won't," I said. "It wasn't even your fault. Can you move your leg? If you can't, it might be broken."

"I've got to get home!" Olivia cried.

Christina and I helped her up. "Let's pull you home on a toboggan," I said. "You should really look at it before you walk on it."

Olivia slapped my hand away. "I'm going home,"

she said, and started walking.

She was hardly limping, which was amazing, considering how hard she'd hit. Christina and I trotted after her.

"You sure you don't want a ride?" Christina asked.

"Leave me alone," said Olivia. She was still sniffling and crying. "And *don't* follow me!"

"But your mom isn't even home," I objected. "What if your leg is all bloody, and you faint at the sight of it, and you're alone on the bathroom floor for an hour?"

Olivia didn't answer me, but we kept following her. It was Christina and I who took her sledding in the first place, and we were going to make sure she was okay before we left her alone.

At her front door, Olivia tried to shut us out, but with two against one, she lost. She ran to the bathroom and locked herself in. We sat down outside the bathroom door and listened to her pulling off her jacket and the snow pants and whimpering, "Mommy's going to kill me!" Then there was quiet, except for sniffles.

"Are you bleeding?" I asked. I figured this was no time to worry about good questions and bad questions.

"No," she said in a small voice.

"Are you hurt bad?" asked Christina.

"No, just medium," said Olivia. She let out a ragged sigh.

"How about we all take our wet stuff off and make sandwiches," I suggested.

"No," said Olivia. "You can go home now."

That really made me mad. We'd been having a great time together, and here she was kicking us out! "Olivia, are you our friend or not?!" I shouted at the bathroom door.

"Yes, I am your friend," came a surprised voice from the bathroom.

"Then why are you being so mean to us?"

"I'm not!" she insisted.

All right, I thought. I guess if you have a hurt leg and you've been crying and you're tired from sledding, then maybe it's normal to want your friends to leave you alone.

"You could at least come out of the bathroom to say good-bye to us," I said.

There was silence, then one sniff. "I can't come out," she said.

Christina and I looked at each other with wide eyes. "Why not?" Christina asked.

More silence. Then: "I can't tell you."

"Why *not?*" I demanded.

Olivia groaned. "Because you won't want to be my friends anymore if I tell you."

Christina and I exchanged a confused look. "Listen, Olivia," I said. "We just *are* your friends. If you're mean to us, it could make us mad, but there isn't anything that could make us stop being your friends, okay?"

We heard nose blowing from the bathroom, then: "But my cousin said American children expect everyone to be perfect, like movie stars."

You should have seen the look Christina and I gave each other over that one.

Olivia continued, "He said that if Americans find out you're not perfect, they won't like you and they'll tease you."

"Believe me, Olivia," I said, "I already *know* you're not perfect. You get mad at me all the time for no good reason, you keep secrets from us, and you won't even play soccer with us at recess. And we still like you. So tell your cousin to chill out, okay?"

"That's not what he meant," said Olivia very softly.

"What?" said Christina, putting her head closer to the door. "Hey, could you at least come out of there so we don't have to yell through the door?"

"I told you, I can't come out," said Olivia.

Then, after we'd all three sat there not knowing

what to say for a minute, she added, "Unless you help me."

"Of course we'll help you!" Christina exclaimed.

Olivia said she needed us to get her some crutches, which were hidden in a pile of clothes under her bed. I was hoping that didn't mean her leg was hurt a lot worse than she'd been telling us. When she opened the bathroom door a crack, we slipped the crutches to her, just like she asked us to.

We heard rustling and a couple of thumps, and then the bathroom door opened. There stood Olivia, her eyes red from crying and her hair wild and wet from melted snow. She balanced on the crutches with her right foot on the floor. The left leg of her sweatpants hung limp. Leaning against the bathroom wall, wearing my old snow boot, stood an artificial leg.

FIVE

"Is *that* why you won't play soccer with us?" I asked.

Olivia nodded. She swung smoothly on her crutches and led us to the kitchen. She plopped down in a chair. Christina and I sat, too, and started pulling off our wet clothes.

"Is that why you miss school sometimes?" Christina asked.

"Yes. I've been going in for appointments for that new leg—it's the whole reason we came to the U.S. First I had to get a plaster cast. Then they fitted it. After I walk on it a few days, I go in and they make it fit even better. It's much nicer than my old one. This one has an ankle that moves, so I can run."

I was full of questions again, and I hoped Olivia wouldn't mind them now that her secret was out.

"How did you lose it?" I asked.

"In an auto accident. It was all crushed from here down." She pressed in on her sweatpants below her knee to show us where her leg ended. "The doctor finally said it had to go."

"How old were you?" asked Christina.

"Eight—two years ago."

I suddenly remembered something. "Hey, you said you were hurt medium-bad—are you okay?"

"Yeah," said Olivia. "It's just that my stump got bruised, and when I took the leg off, my stump swelled up and now I can't fit the leg back on. I'll miss school again tomorrow."

"Why don't you just come in on crutches?" Christina asked.

"And have everyone stare at me? No way! That's why I was so relieved about not having to wear a school uniform with a skirt. I can hide my leg all year under long pants."

"Once everyone saw it, they'd get used to it," I said.

"They'd tease me," she insisted.

"Mr. Harrison wouldn't let them," I said.

Olivia shook her head as if I was crazy. "I am *not* showing the whole school that I have an artificial leg."

I decided not to argue with her, but I still had a few questions. "Olivia, if you weren't hurt much, why were you crying so hard?"

"Because that leg cost a fortune! My father had to borrow a pile of money to pay for it, and if I'd broken it, I think both of my parents would have had heart attacks."

"So is it okay?" Christina asked.

Olivia grinned. "That duvet for my bum you gave me—what do you call it, snow pants? That was good protection. It's not even dented."

I was happy I'd done something to help.

"You said this new leg has an ankle so you can run?" I asked.

"Yeah," she said.

"Does it have a foot so you can kick, too?"

"Sure," she said.

"Then *why* won't you play soccer with us?" I demanded.

Olivia looked down at her hands in her lap. "Because when I run, I look funny. People might figure it out."

"Figure what out?" asked Christina.

"About the leg."

I threw my hands up in exasperation. "So just come to school tomorrow on crutches, tell the whole story, and then when you can get the leg back on, you can play soccer and nobody will wonder why you run funny."

Olivia made a face like she'd just eaten rotten fish.

● ● ●

It turns out snow doesn't act the same way in Maryland as it does in Maine. In Maryland it disappears fast. By Monday morning, there were bare spots on the grass where people had walked or kids had gathered snow for snowballs. By the time we got out of school, the birds were singing and you could hardly even tell we'd had a snowstorm. Christina was disappointed that it had snowed on a Saturday night so we didn't even get a day off from school.

"So, next time it will probably snow on a Wednesday or something," I said as we walked home.

Christina laughed. "It's almost spring break, silly. It won't snow again."

What did I know? I'd just gotten a letter from my best friend back in Maine, Andrea, and she said there was two feet of snow everywhere.

"What are you doing for spring break?" Christina asked.

In Maine, for spring break we used to travel some-where warmer. Here, that hardly seemed necessary. "My parents aren't planning a trip or anything," I said.

"Mine neither," said Christina. She raised her eyebrows. "Don't you think it's time we talk them into one?"

"How about one in which they take you and me and Olivia with them?" I suggested.

"Yes!" Christina spun around. "One in which we go camping!"

"And to an amusement park!" I chimed in.

"And to the beach!" Christina threw her arms into the air, which at that moment was feeling very springtimey, even though there were little piles of snow lying around.

We decided to each work on our parents and see which one we could convince that taking off from work for a trip was a terrific idea. Spring break, Christina informed me, was only three weeks away.

We brought Olivia her schoolwork. She was still getting around on crutches. We told her about our spring-break plan, and she promised she'd talk to her mother, as well. Out of five parents, we figured we had a pretty good chance of getting to go some-place.

By Wednesday, when I had to ride my bike to basketball practice, it was so warm I didn't even mind the wind on my ears. Doug greeted me with a basketball in my face, and the coach made us do drills and scrimmages and yelled at us the whole time.

"You've got to run *harder!*" he shouted. "Fight for that score! You need a killer instinct if you're going to win!" And then, toward the end, he yelled, "You're a bunch of girls, you know that?"

I got a little worried about him when he said that, because I'd already noticed that I was the only girl on the team. "Is the coach nearsighted?" I asked Doug.

He gave me a blank look. "Don't worry about all

the yelling," he said. "He'd just like us to win a game before the season is over, and he thinks insults will make us play harder."

"What insults?" I asked, but Doug had to jump up because he got called into a scrimmage.

I was really tired by the time I rode my bike home. I dragged myself into the kitchen and plopped down with Jerod at the kitchen table. He had that party invitation from Sheila in front of him.

"Dapartyznegs weekend," he said, like he was announcing a funeral or something.

"You sound really excited," I said.

He screwed up his face. "If I knew what 'come as you are' meant, I'd be excited."

"What did Mom say it means?"

"Didn't ask."

I rolled my eyes. "So ask her as soon as she gets home," I said.

We raided the cheese and crackers and orange

juice, and the minute my mom walked in the door, I called, "Hey, Mom, Jerod has a question for you," so he couldn't get out of it.

Jerod blushed, but he showed her the invitation. Mom said "come as you are" just means that whatever you were wearing when you got the invitation —your jeans and a sweater or sweatshirt—would be fine to wear to the party. It means you don't have to get dressed up.

I gave her a very serious look. "What if you went out to get the mail real early in your pajamas? Are you supposed to wear your pajamas to the party?"

"It's not that literal, Sarah—" Mom began.

"Or what if Jerod was in the shower and I saw this letter from Sheila and I knew he'd want to see it right away, so I handed it to him through the shower curtain. Is he supposed to go to the party with no—"

"Sarah!" Mom interrupted me, which was probably a good thing because Jerod's face was turning lots of shades of red. "It just means you can come the way you normally dress, okay? It means you don't have to wear anything special or rent a tuxedo or try to look different than you usually look. Do you understand?"

I said I understood. But I liked the idea of sending out party invitations that say "come as you are" and having everybody show up looking just the way they did when they opened the invitation—bed head, Noxzema all over their face, nothing on but a towel, or whatever.

SIX

Saturday's game was at another church. I left my bike in the bike stand and got a ride in a mini-van full of noisy boys. Coach was grumpy, as usual, but Doug said he thought we could win this one because of our new players and because the team we were playing had lost all of their games so far, too.

I felt kind of responsible, being one of the new players. While we did warmups, I got myself psyched up to do defense like a maniac. I decided the person I got paired with would see nothing but my hand coming down in their face. I guess I was developing that "killer instinct" the coach said we needed.

"Gajeski, I want you in first string," Coach shouted. "And get your head out of the clouds."

I guess I looked like I was daydreaming. I would have told him that's just what my face looks like while it's developing a killer instinct, but I didn't want to annoy him any further.

I got paired up with a short kid who looked like he'd eaten too many doughnuts. Defense was easy, and I was pretty sure I was making him good and mad. He never even got close to scoring. When I was on offense, he couldn't stop me. Not only had my sneakers grown little hovercraft rockets, but it seemed like my team members thought I was the person to pass to, especially with Doughnut Boy lagging behind me all the time. I crammed it in from the right, the left, and even made a three-pointer. During halftime, the coach slapped me on the back and said, "Way to go, Gajeski!" Doug and a bunch of the other guys high-fived me.

When we went back in, I had to guard a different guy who was taller and skinnier and made it a lot harder for me to score. I didn't do nearly as well in the second half, but my teammates had it in their heads that I was the star, and when the game was over and we'd won, they gave me a heaping share of the credit.

We went out for pizza, and the coach looked happy for a change. He even stood up with his Coke and made a toast to "A great team. A great bunch of guys." I was relieved to find out someone had finally told him the team was mostly boys.

My only disappointment was that my mom and dad hadn't seen me be a star. I did use that to my advantage, though. Christina's parents had both already said they couldn't afford the time off from work for a spring-break trip, and Olivia's mom said she didn't know enough about the United States to take three young girls "on holiday," so my folks were the only ones left to convince. I thought a little guilt might just do the trick.

Anytime there was a lull in the conversation at the dinner table, I took the opportunity to rub it in.

"You should have seen me! I was unstoppable. All the parents were cheering—except you, of course, because you weren't there."

My mom felt really bad because her boss had already said she couldn't take any vacation time until the summer, so I let up on her after a while. But I figured my dad could just tell his customers the new toilet or new floor would have to wait because he was going away. By the time I finished begging, he said he'd take me and my friends, and Jerod if he wanted to go, camping at the beach for a long weekend, *and* he said he'd come to next Saturday's game!

Olivia, Christina, and I started planning the trip right away. "Maybe we can go to Virginia Beach," said Christina. "It'll be warmer there than Ocean City, and they've got a campground."

"How about an amusement park?" I asked.

"Right on the beach," said Christina.

Olivia was twisting the edge of her shirt. "How about a bathtub?" she asked quietly.

"What for?" I asked.

She threw her hands up. "To take a bath in! What else would it be for?"

"It's *camping*," I said. "That's the fun of it. You stay dirty."

Olivia gave me a wide smile.

We planned our packing list, which included an extra sleeping bag for Olivia, and no bathing suits because even in Virginia in April you'd have to be a polar bear to get in the ocean.

On Tuesday evening, my dad took the three of us to Hudson Trail Outfitters to get camping stuff, like kerosene for the lantern and freeze-dried food. My dad likes camping, but he doesn't like cooking, so packages that say "add water and stir" are as fancy as we get on camping trips.

Olivia picked out lasagna, and I was looking at the slab of shriveled-up aluminum foil, trying to figure out how it was supposed to pouffe up into a nice big tray of lasagna, when I heard, "Yo, Sam."

It was Doug.

"Hi. What are you doing here?" I asked, as if he was allowed to exist only at basketball practice or games and was supposed to evaporate at all other times.

"My dad is shopping for a kayak, and he dragged me along," he said. Then his eyes sparkled, and he jerked his chin toward Christina and Olivia. They were rummaging through the piles of dehydrated gourmet food. "So introduce me, huh?" he said.

"Oh, yeah. Hey, you guys, this is Doug from my basketball team. That's Christina and that's Olivia."

The girls turned and said, "Wassup?" but then went back to a discussion about whether chicken cordon bleu would taste any less like cardboard than boeuf bourguignon, considering the fact that both of them look like dried mice before you add water.

Doug nudged me. "Hey, bring them to a game sometime, okay?"

"Sure. If they want to come."

His father called him. Doug said, "Later," and left.

We got the chicken and the beef, along with the lasagna, since we needed three dinners anyway.

At practice on Wednesday, I told Doug how my dad was actually coming to the next game.

"Awesome," he said. "And what about the babes?"

"The *what?*"

"Those girls you were with at the store. Did you get them to come, too?"

I couldn't believe he'd called them babes. I just stared at him with an angry look, which he didn't seem to notice.

"I'd love to have a couple of girls that pretty cheering for me while I'm out on the court!" he said.

"Get your own cheering section," I snapped. "They're my friends, and they're not *babes.*" I said "babes" like it was a cat mess on the kitchen floor.

"Geez, would you chill?" he said.

Coach told me to guard Doug. I was so mad, I made him look like Doughnut Boy on the court. I'm not sure if I was madder at him for acting so ridiculous about girls, for calling my friends such a stupid name, or for *not* calling *me* that same stupid name, but I was mad enough to block every one of his shots all afternoon.

"Whoa," he said when practice was over. "You're getting really good."

All I said was, "See you Saturday," and I hurried out the door to my bicycle.

Friday evening, Jerod took at least two hours to get ready for Sheila's party. He showered and put gel in his hair, which was still mostly black but had blond roots growing out because he said he was tired of dyeing it. Then he started choosing clothes, and by the looks of the pile he left on his bed, he'd tried on every pair of jeans and every sweater he owned before deciding on the right "come as you are" combination.

When Mom was ready to drive Jerod and his friend Phil to the party, she wouldn't let me come because she said Jerod was nervous and didn't need his little sister gawking and making things worse. I asked her if I could wait up for him with her so I could hear all about the party. She finally said I could, since Phil's father would be bringing Jerod home by 11:00, and I'm always too wound up the night before a game to get to sleep much before then, anyway.

So, when Jerod walked in the door at 11:05 p.m., wearing a pair of teal green sweatpants that barely reached his calves and a gray-and-pink sweatshirt, Mom and I both wanted an explanation.

"Where are your clothes?" I demanded.

"At Sheila's. She was too embarrassed to let me wash them."

"And *why* do they need to be washed?" Mom asked, giving him a suspicious look.

"She threw up on them."

"Poor girl," Mom said, no longer suspicious. "Is she coming down with a stomach virus?"

"No," said Jerod. "It was because of the beer."

Mom's eyes bulged, and I blurted out, "You were drinking beer?"

Jerod shook his head emphatically. "No way. We weren't. Her schnauzer was."

I narrowed my eyes at him. "Let me get this straight. Sheila's dog was drinking beer, and that made Sheila throw up?"

"Yeah," said Jerod, nodding as if he was thankful that someone finally understood. "It wouldn't have happened if the police hadn't come, though."

Mom went pale. "The police?" she asked weakly.

"Yeah. When the police came to the door and Sheila's dad went to answer it, he left his can of beer on the kitchen table. The dog jumped up, knocked the beer over, drank the part that spilled, and then came downstairs where the party was and threw up all over the carpet. Sheila took one look and threw up all over me. I didn't blame her. It made me gag, too."

I was thinking, *Wow, Sheila threw up on him and he still likes her,* but Mom had other concerns. "Jerod," she said sternly, "could you please explain to me why the police were at this party?"

"Yeah. One of the neighbors called because of the screaming."

By now, Mom was rubbing her forehead as if this was giving her a big headache. "And where was Sheila's mother during all of this?" she asked.

"Before the police got there, or afterward?" Jerod wanted to know.

"Let's start with before," said Mom.

"I guess she must have been cleaning out the fireplace."

"I see. And after the police got there?" Mom was working really hard at staying calm.

"That's when she was mopping up the spilled beer

and asking the policemen if they would please get the bats off the bathroom curtains, which is where they'd gone after they flew down the chimney and right into her face, which is why she'd been screaming."

Mom sighed with relief. "Is there anything else about this party I should know?" she asked.

Jerod thought a moment. "Just that police won't get bats out of your bathroom for you. You have to call Animal Control."

Mom nodded. "That's good information to have."

I followed Jerod up to his room. "So how was the *party?*" I asked.

He shrugged. "It was cool. We ate chips and drank soda, listened to music and played video games. No big deal."

I hope the first boy-girl party I go to is that exciting.

By Saturday, I was in a great mood because my dad was coming to the game with me. We didn't even stop at the parking lot to pick up other kids. We just drove, the two of us, and talked about game strategies and the camping trip, and I filled him in on Jerod's adventures at Sheila's party the night before, since he was already asleep when Jerod got home.

I wouldn't say I was a big star of the game. The other team's coach figured out I was pretty good, so instead of getting a short, fat kid to guard, I got a tall guy with knuckles down to his knees. But I still drove in 20 of our winning 62 points, and that was plenty to get me celebrity status for the day. You should have heard my dad yelling and cheering. I thought he was going to have laryngitis for a week. When the game was over, Dad picked me up and swung me around. "Sarah, you're the best!" he said.

The coach was on his way out with the crowd, but as he passed us, he gave my dad a slap on the back and called out, "You must be very proud of your son!"

That's when I *really* started to hate bubble gum.

SEVEN

"Is the coach nearsighted?" asked my dad.

"*Nooo,*" I groaned. "I think," I said slowly, "there has been"—I rubbed my forehead—"a mistake."

Dad walked me to the car with his arm around my shoulders. "There were no girls on the other team," he said, as if either of us needed more evidence of what was going on.

"I heard a couple of the parents talking about the girls' league schedule. I just never thought about it much," I said.

My dad suddenly brightened. "There's no problem here. You made the boys' league, and you're one of the best players. So who's to complain?"

I looked at him with sad puppy eyes. "I'm in the

boys' league and I'm a girl. I think that's a problem, Dad."

"Naw. Just let your coach in on the secret at the next practice. I'm sure he'll be fine with it."

I wasn't so sure. I thought it was more likely he'd kick me off the team and yell at me some while he was doing it.

On the way home, we kept the conversation away from basketball. I had this bad feeling, like a dark cloud had settled on all the fun I'd been having as a star player on my team.

By Wednesday's practice, I'd decided not to tell anybody anything. It wasn't my fault there'd been a misunderstanding. It wasn't my problem nobody had ever noticed that I used the girls' room rather than the boys' room. Why tattle and spoil all my fun? There only a couple of games left, anyway, because there were none during spring break.

Right when I was feeling good about letting

everyone go on thinking I was a boy, the coach made an announcement.

"We've been invited to play a team up in Pennsylvania. I've got permission slips here for your parents to sign. The game is in two and a half weeks. We'll leave on a bus from the church parking lot on Friday evening and arrive home late Saturday night."

Everybody cheered. One kid raised his hand. "Do we get to stay at a hotel?"

Coach shook his head. "The church up there has a bunkhouse for their summer camp we can use. Bring a sleeping bag, soap, and a towel. They've got a nice big locker-room shower. I'm going to throw every single one of you in there after the game. I'm not riding home with a bunch of smelly kids."

I almost fainted.

The other kids started shouting things like "Pennsylvania, here we come!" and "Yippee! We get to travel just like a real team!"

I sat there wondering where I could hide while the coach was throwing everybody in the shower.

When my mom got home from work that night, she asked, "What did the coach say when you told him?"

"Nothing," I mumbled.

"He didn't say anything at all?" she asked, surprised.

"No," I said. "I told him nothing."

Before she could lecture me on Being Truthful About Your Gender, I figured I'd better get the permission slip out of the way. "It'll be okay," I said. "We only have a couple of games left and one of them is in Pennsylvania, so I just need you to sign a permission slip and write a note that says I have a highly contagious skin disease, so I can't take a shower in the locker room with the rest of the team."

Mom looked a little pale.

"*Please*, Mom?" I begged. "I don't want to get kicked

off the team. Not now, before this big Pennsylvania game. I'm going to get to *travel*, just like the pros!"

Now she looked mad. "Sarah, I won't have you masquerading around as a boy on a trip to another state."

I sighed. "Never mind. If you won't sign the permission slip, it doesn't matter, anyway." I tried to look as disappointed as I felt.

"I'll sign the slip if it says 'Sarah' on it," she said, and put her hand on my cheek.

I shook my head. If the coach knew I was Sarah and not Sam, I was sure he wouldn't let me go.

"Sarah, honey, pretending to be someone you're not is just like lying. It's much better—for everyone—to be honest about who you are. Just present them with the naked truth."

"Mom!" I cried. "I am *not* taking a shower with all those boys!"

"Did I say something about a shower?" she asked, confused.

"You said 'naked.'"

She laughed. "The naked *truth*. That means you should be honest. Be yourself. Remember Jerod's invitation to Sheila's party?"

I nodded.

"It's kind of like 'come as you are.' Come as yourself, not as something—or someone—you're not."

Mom was making a lot of sense. There was one problem: the truth was, I was a girl, and the coach wasn't about to let a girl travel to Pennsylvania with the boys' team. But all I really had to do was change my name to "Sarah" on the permission slip, have my mom sign it, change it back to Sam before I gave it to the coach, and then disappear during shower-time. It wasn't exactly the naked truth, but it was a way to get to travel like the pros and play a couple more games as a star.

I told my mom, "Thanks," and gave her a hug. I really did appreciate her advice. I just wasn't going to follow it.

•   •   •

The good news was, I wouldn't even be seeing the coach until after spring break, and on Saturday we were heading to Virginia Beach—me, Christina, Olivia, my dad, and a whole pile of camping equipment. Jerod had decided not to go with us because he said there were too many fifth-grade girls going.

Saturday morning was sunny and so warm my mom's daffodils bloomed. I put on some shorts and threw an extra pair into my backpack.

We drove by Christina's and then Olivia's and loaded their stuff into the car. They were both as excited as I was. The three of us sat in the back-seat and left my dad to enjoy himself singing along with oldies on the radio. We talked about what we wanted to do when we got to the beach. We were in agreement about the first stop: any amusement park with a roller coaster.

We got hamburgers and sodas for lunch, but

since my dad wanted to keep driving, we ate in the car. I managed to spill my soda all over Olivia's jeans.

Olivia looked down at her soaked pants and groaned. "I didn't bring another pair," she said.

"We can wash them at the campsite and hang them to dry," Christina suggested.

"Okay," said Olivia.

"You can borrow my shorts for now," I said. "I've got extra, and it's too hot for jeans anyway."

Olivia got that worried look she used to get when I asked her too many questions. "Shorts?" she squeaked.

Christina and I both knew what she was thinking.

"There won't be anyone from school there," said Christina. "Remember when Mr. Harrison asked where we were going for spring break and nobody else said Virginia Beach except us?"

"Yes, but—" Olivia began.

"Come on, just show the world the naked truth!" I blurted out.

They both stared at me.

"I mean, wouldn't you be more comfortable in shorts? It's getting so hot."

"I guess I would," said Olivia. "And since there won't be anyone from school there . . ." She smiled uncertainly. "Okay."

We pulled over at a rest stop. Christina waited in the car with Dad while I went into the ladies' room with Olivia and my extra shorts. Olivia took off the sticky jeans. It was the first time I'd seen her artificial leg *on*. The stump of her own leg had a thin white sock pulled over it and slid into the top of the artificial leg kind of like it was a slip-on shoe. The artificial leg was held to her own leg with a Velcro strap that wrapped over the top of her knee and around the back of her leg and then fastened. It was really a pretty neat contraption, with "skin" the color of hers, and a foot and an ankle that bent and everything.

"I know my mother called and told your father all

about the leg because of this trip," said Olivia, "but do you think he'll be shocked to see it, just the same?"

"*My* dad? Shocked? Not a chance. He's terminally mellow," I assured her.

When Olivia was done changing, I said, "Here, let me carry those." I took the jeans from her, then ran to the rest room door to hold it open for her.

Olivia stood looking at me with her arms crossed. "All of a sudden I can't do anything for myself?" she asked.

"I—I just thought I'd help," I said. Here she was getting mad at me again, and I had no idea what I was doing wrong.

"You didn't think I needed this much help when you couldn't see my leg," she said bluntly.

I let go of the door, and it swung shut with a clang. She was right.

"Sorry," I said. I handed her back the jeans.

"If you think I need help, just ask me, okay?"

"Sure," I said.

"And please don't decide what kind of help I need," she said. "If I say, 'Yes, I need help,' then ask me *how* you can help and I'll tell you."

"Okay. Do you need any help now?" I asked.

She rolled her eyes. "I didn't need any help getting in here, why should I need help getting out?" she said, but she wasn't mad.

She opened the door for both of us, and we stepped into the bright sunshine.

"Thanks for the shorts," she said. "It *is* getting hot, and I didn't bring any."

A sea gull flew overhead and squawked. "I think we're almost there!" I shouted.

We decided to go to the beach before our campsite. Olivia said she missed the beach a lot because in Trinidad she had lived only a few blocks away from it. We figured we'd take a walk and collect shells. Then, when we found a place to park, we also found an amusement park, complete with a roller coaster. It wasn't a big one, like the one

Christina said they had near the boardwalk, but it had a Ferris wheel and bumper cars and lots of other fun-looking stuff, and it was set up almost right on the beach, so we'd have a view of the ocean from every ride.

It didn't take much begging to get my dad to hand us each a couple of dollars. He said we could find him napping in the car when we were through being whirled and bumped and spun around.

We bought tickets and ran straight for the roller coaster, but there was a line.

"Let's try that thing," said Christina. She pointed to a ride that was yanking people in about eight different directions.

"Cool," I said.

Olivia agreed.

When it was our turn, we piled onto the ride, and the three of us squashed into one molded red seat. It was really noisy with the roller coaster clacking nearby, and people squealing and yelling, and a shooting range going off like fireworks, and the waves rumbling in the background. When the pimply-faced teenage kid who was in charge of the ride came by to lock us in with the bar, Olivia was leaning over. The guy made her sit up so he could pull the safety bar down and snap it into place. She said something about a strap, but I couldn't really hear her over all the racket, and the next thing I knew, we lifted off.

We spun and then whipped, then zoomed down, then up. We got twirled in so many directions I didn't think I'd ever walk straight again. I could hear Christina screaming louder than anybody. I think she *really* likes amusement parks.

When the ride finally stopped, Christina and I were both laughing, and it took us a minute to realize that Olivia wasn't. She looked stunned, and even through her dark skin I could see that she'd turned pale. "Olivia, do you feel sick?" I asked loudly, over all the noise.

She shook her head and frowned. "I needed to fix the strap. It had come undone," she said.

I had no idea what she was talking about. Christina looked down, her eyes got real wide, and she grabbed my arm and shook it hard. I looked down and went pale myself. Olivia's artificial leg was gone.

"My mother is going to kill me!" Olivia wailed.

Everyone was piling off the ride and clambering by us.

"We'll go find it," said Christina quickly.

"It's broken for sure!" Olivia cried. "She'll never let me leave the house again."

The kid in charge of the ride shouted at us, "Hey, you can't ride again without paying. Get out of there."

Christina and I shoved the bar up and tried to get Olivia out of the seat. We were all awkward, pulling at different times, and it wasn't working. Suddenly, I remembered something. "Olivia, *do you need help?*" I asked.

"Yes!" she exclaimed.

"*How* can we help you?" I asked.

She thought for a moment. "You can both be my crutches. Lift up under my arms, and I can hop and lean on you."

Christina and I counted one, two, three, and lifted at the same time. We each put an arm around Olivia and let her put her weight on us for each hop.

As we went past the pimply-faced teenage kid, he said, "You go to the end of the line if you want to ride again."

I glared at him. "She lost something, dude," I said, and pointed to Olivia.

If he'd had false teeth, they would have dropped onto the pavement. We left him to freak out by himself.

It wasn't easy, with the three of us traveling that way, and once we got to a bench next to the ride, Olivia said, "Just leave me here and go find it, *please?*"

"You want me to get my dad?" I asked.

"No," she wailed. "Just find my leg!"

We helped her sit down, then Christina and I both ran to look around under the ride. The leg wasn't there.

"It must have gotten thrown—that ride was whipping us around so hard," said Christina.

I cringed. I hoped like crazy it hadn't been damaged. "Okay. You go that way, I'll go this way," I said, and we ran off in different directions.

I jostled through the crowd. I searched everywhere I could think of—between the feet of people standing in line for the roller coaster, on top of the canopy over the cotton-candy booth, even behind the trash bin. No leg.

When I got to the edge of the little amusement park, where the blacktop ended and the sandy beach began, there was a tight knot of people gathered around something. I had a pretty good idea what it was.

I shoved between the people, and sure enough, there was Olivia's leg lying in the sand. Next to it was this big lifeguard-type guy, flat on his back with his eyes closed. Kneeling over him, fanning his face with her pink-fingernailed hands, was a teenage girl in short-shorts and a bathing-suit top. "We were just walking along," the girl was saying breathlessly, "and this . . . *leg* landed, and he—he fainted dead away!" She sniffled and looked up at the worried faces.

I didn't stay to watch more. I snatched up the leg.

"I know who this belongs to," I said real loud, and elbowed my way out of the crowd just as the guy started groaning and blinking his eyes.

I ran back to Olivia. A little kid with round brown eyes was sitting next to her, swinging his legs and sucking on two fingers.

"Does it hurt?" I heard him ask.

"No," said Olivia. "Not anymore."

"But where are your *toes?*" he asked.

Olivia laughed. "You've got ten toes, and I've got five, I suppose."

I sat down with them and handed her the leg. "Mission accomplished," I said.

Olivia gasped. "Is it all right?" she asked, examining it.

"It looks fine to me," I said. "It landed in the sand."

"Oh, thank you, thank you, thank you!" Olivia cried.

I think that was two thank yous to me for finding her leg, and one to the sand for catching it.

"There's your other toes!" the little boy said as he watched Olivia put the leg back on and retie the sneaker that covered the foot.

Olivia smiled at him.

"Daniel, what are you *doing?*" A woman yanked the kid off the bench. "Don't bother those people," she snapped. She gave Olivia a weirded-out glance and turned away.

The boy waved to Olivia, and she waved back as his mother dragged him off.

Olivia patted the leg. "What a relief!" she exclaimed.

"Wait till you hear about the excitement it caused," I said.

When Christina came back, I told them how that big, handsome hulking guy had passed out cold when Olivia's leg came flying through the air, and how his girlfriend looked like she was about to faint, too, just to get more attention from the crowd. We laughed so hard we had tears running down our faces.

"I wish I could have seen it," said Olivia.

"Me, too," said Christina.

Before we got on the roller coaster, Olivia made sure her strap was fastened good and tight.

EIGHT

That evening at the campsite, we managed to get our tents set up before dark—one for my dad and one for the three of us. We made the lasagna in a pot on the kerosene stove. It turned out to be a lump of lasagna instead of a tray of lasagna, but it tasted pretty good anyway.

After dinner, my dad said if we gathered enough wood, he'd build a campfire and we could roast the marshmallows we'd brought. Christina and Olivia and I tromped through the woods in the dark, picking up sticks and branches. Once, I grabbed a stick with a slug on it and thought it was a snake. I screeched and dropped the stick. Nobody wanted to pick up any more wood after that, but my dad said we had enough.

We sat on logs in a circle, with the fire making our faces glow. My dad told all the scary stories he remembered from when he was a kid. They weren't very scary, which was nice, because the woods were really dark.

We toasted and ate the whole bag of marshmallows. Then Olivia, Christina, and I brushed our teeth at the water spigot and spit right on the ground, made one more stop at the outhouse, and crawled into our tent. I heard the Velcro crackle as Olivia took off her leg, then a thump as she set it down next to her in the tent. We each snuggled into our sleeping bags.

"It was a great day," said Christina.

"Awesome," I said.

"It was the best," said Olivia.

That was it for the talking. I think we were all asleep in about ten seconds.

The first thing I remember hearing the next morning

was a loud unzipping sound. The second thing was my dad's footsteps moving around our campsite and snapping twigs in the woods behind our tent. The third was him saying, "Oh dear. Oh my. Oh *no!*"

I sat up. Christina and Olivia were still asleep. I unzipped our tent and stuck my head out.

"Dad," I whispered loudly. "What's the matter?"

"You girls went into the woods over here to gather sticks last night, right?"

I nodded.

He rubbed his forehead. "Oh dear. Oh my."

"What is it?" I squeaked. I crawled out of my tent and walked barefoot over to where he was standing, looking at the ground.

There were no big leaves on the trees yet, just lots of buds and some small leaves. The forest floor was covered with light green ferns, May apples, and blue wildflowers. It was really pretty. I couldn't figure out what he was oh-no-ing about.

Dad crouched down and pointed to a short sprig

coming out of the ground with tiny leaves sprouting from it. Tiny, shiny leaves with notches on them. In groups of three.

"Oh no," I said. "Oh dear."

"Oh my," he said.

"We better get in the shower," I said.

"Right away," he said.

I went back to our tent and jostled Christina's foot.

"Hey, you guys, wake up. We got into poison ivy last night."

Olivia stretched and yawned. "What's poison ivy?" she asked.

Christina groaned. "It makes you bumpy and swollen and itchy for weeks if you get it."

"But if we wash really well right now, we probably won't get it," I hurried to add.

Olivia pulled her sleeping bag up over her head.

"You can't stay in bed, Olivia," I insisted. "The sooner we wash it off, the better."

"You said there was no bathtub," came a small voice from inside the sleeping bag.

"No, but there's showers," I said.

There was a moment of silence from the sleeping bag. Then, "How bad is the itching?"

"*Really* bad," said Christina. "Believe me, you don't want to get it."

"It was going to be fun to stay dirty, but we can get dirty again after the shower," I suggested.

Christina and I were already gathering our clothes, but Olivia hadn't budged.

"I'm sure my dad has extra towels and soap we can use," I offered. Christina and I stared at the unmoving sleeping bag, then at each other.

"Come on, Olivia, let's go," Christina tried to coax her.

She still didn't answer or move.

"Olivia, do you need help?" I asked softly.

I wasn't positive, but I thought her head nodded under the sleeping bag.

"*How* can we help?" I asked.

She peeked out. "I don't know." She sounded close to tears. "But I can't take showers. I can't get the leg wet or it will be ruined, and I can't balance on a wet shower floor on one leg. I'll fall."

I sat on a pile of clothes to think. "What if we hold you up—act like your crutches, the way we did yesterday?"

"The showers are big," said Christina. "I saw them yesterday. There's plenty of room for all three of us in there." Her face was lit up, like the whole thing was going to be fun instead of a problem. "We'll make sure you don't fall."

Olivia sat up. "I think that might work," she said hopefully.

"We'll save water," I said.

"It'll be like a party!" said Christina.

And that's exactly what we sounded like—a great big party in the shower, with our voices echoing off the tile walls and our giggling getting louder every time we splashed each other. Olivia held on real tight to Christina with one arm and to the soap dish with her other hand. I washed her legs—both the long one and the short one—with a soapy washcloth until I was sure there was no more poison ivy on them. I even had to wash her hands and arms for her, because she was having to concentrate so hard on not falling.

After I'd scrubbed my own arms and legs, I held Olivia up so that Christina could wash herself. After that we really started having fun. We filled our mouths up with water and spouted it like whales. We got our hair all sudsy and made it stick straight out. We threw our washcloths at the ceiling and tried to make them stick. And Christina showed us how you can get your palms real soapy, cup your hands together, and blow at your thumbs to make huge bubbles come out from between your pinkies. Then we named ourselves the Three Naked Musketeers and shouted, "One for all! And all for one!" at the top of our lungs because we liked the way it echoed. I've never had so much fun in the shower in my life.

I think we annoyed most of the ladies who wanted to take a shower that morning because when we finally came out, they were lined up with their soap and shampoo and with very grumpy looks on their faces.

NINE

The rest of the camping weekend was terrific, with a trip to the big amusement park, shopping and eating junk food along the boardwalk, making a sand castle on the beach, and cooking and washing dishes at the campsite. It's funny how when you're camping, even washing dishes or brushing your teeth can be fun because you're doing it outside.

The rest of spring break was great, too. Christina and I got Olivia to play soccer with us in Christina's backyard. She did kind of limp when she ran, but she was a pretty good player. We bugged her some more about playing soccer with us at school, but she still didn't want to hear about it.

Then came the first week of school after spring

break, which wasn't nearly as much fun as the vacation had been. I wasn't sure if it was just school that put me in a bad mood, or the fact that basketball practice was coming up on Wednesday. I knew that on Wednesday I'd have to either tell the coach the truth or do some dishonest name changing on my permission slip for Pennsylvania.

On Monday afternoon, Christina came back to Mr. Harrison's room from her Social Studies class looking like she was ready to strangle somebody.

"Mrs. Green is ignorant and mean!" she announced.

"What did she do?" asked Olivia.

Christina's eyes flashed. "She's got her mind set and won't listen to me."

I knew enough not to bug Christina when she was this mad.

Jamal arrived back from the same Social Studies group and sat down at his place. "That pageant sounds cool, huh, Christina?" he asked cheerfully.

I thought Christina might hit him. "No, it does *not* sound cool!" she snapped.

Jamal put up his hands in self-defense. "Hey, I thought it sounded all right. I get to represent North Carolina because that's where my grandparents are from, so I thought that was neat. No big deal. Sorry you don't like it." He started organizing his papers.

"So, do I get to represent El Salvador because that's where my grandparents *and* parents are from? Or even Maryland, because that's where *I'm* from? No! I get to represent Mexico! Everybody else gets to represent the state or country their family is from, and Mrs. Green is making me come out on stage and talk about *Mexico!*"

"It's just a pageant," said Jamal.

I winced.

Christina got up in his face. "If it's just a pageant, then why don't *you* do Mexico?!"

Jamal balked. "I don't have any relatives from Mexico. I want to do North Carolina."

Christina brought her fist down on her desk. "And *I* want to do El Salvador!"

"Did you tell her?" I asked timidly.

"Yes!" Christina was getting awfully loud. It was a good thing the rest of the class was talking, waiting for the time to leave for gym, so our group wasn't getting in trouble for causing a commotion. "And do you know what she said? She has this great costume she bought in Mexico, and she wants me to wear it because I'd look 'perfect.' I told her it's not my country, and she said all those countries down there are so close together, why was I making such a big deal out of it."

"That's not fair," said Olivia.

"Especially if everybody else got to choose the place their family is really from," I added.

"*Everybody* else," said Christina. She glared at Jamal.

"Hey, I'm just doing what the teacher told me to," he said, squirming.

"Is the pageant just for your Social Studies group?" I asked.

"No! It's in the evening, and our parents are invited to come, and everybody will get dressed up." She frowned. "And I've been getting C's in Social Studies all year, and my father wants me to try to get a B on my next report card." She hung her head. "So I guess I'd better do a good job of looking Mexican," she grumbled.

None of us knew what to say.

"I hate Mrs. Green," said Christina.

Then it was time to go to gym.

Christina, Olivia, and I walked home together. Christina was still fuming.

"If I wasn't worried about my grade, I'd tell her it's not fair and I'm not doing it," said Christina.

"That wouldn't be good, either," said Olivia. "Then you'd be left out of a fun pageant."

There didn't seem to be any solution to

Christina's problem, so I decided to make her feel better by talking about my problem with the basketball team.

"Anybody have any whiteout?" I asked. "I've got to change the name on my permission slip for Pennsylvania."

They both stopped walking and stared at me. When I'd first told them about the whole thing, they thought the shower risk was too scary and I should just confess to being a girl and miss the game. That's because neither of them knew how much fun it was to play.

"Sarah, you can't do that," Christina objected. "You'd have to sleep in a bunkhouse with all those boys. And what about the shower?"

"I'll figure something out," I said defensively. "Sometimes you just have to pretend to be something you're not. Like you pretending to be Mexican so you can get a good grade."

Boy, was that the wrong thing to say. Christina

looked like she wanted to tie me into a knot. "That's *different*," she said through clenched teeth.

I think Olivia didn't want us to fight, so she invited us over to her house. "I want to change out of these sweaty clothes," she said. The afternoon was very warm, with a bright, hot sun and not much of a breeze.

Olivia let us come in her room with her while she changed clothes. Since our camping trip, she wasn't self-conscious about her leg around us anymore. Christina and I flopped down on her bed. Olivia took off her long-sleeved shirt and put on a T-shirt. Then she took off her jeans and put on a pair of sweatpants.

"I hope these are cooler," she said.

"Ever heard of *shorts*?" I asked. I hated to keep nagging her, but pretty soon it would be 95 degrees in the shade, and she'd have to either wear shorts or die of heat stroke.

"You haven't even given the kids in class a

chance," said Christina. "I think they'd be really nice and polite."

Olivia fanned herself. "But I only have one chance," she said. "And what if you're wrong? What if they're mean, and talk about me behind my back, and treat me like I'm weird?"

"They *won't*," I insisted. "Listen, Olivia, it's like you're putting on an act. Why don't you just be yourself and trust that everything will be okay?"

"Yeah," Christina agreed. "Stop trying to be something you're not."

Olivia started laughing. Christina and I didn't get what was funny, but Olivia thought something we'd said was hysterical. I don't like feeling left out of a joke, so I blurted out, "What's so funny?!"

Olivia grinned at me. "Look who's talking," she said.

"Huh?"

"Look who's talking about pretending and putting on an act, and trying to be something you're not, just so you can get what you want."

I squirmed. Christina cleared her throat. The room was very quiet for a few minutes.

"My mom says life is like a party with an invitation that says, 'Come as you are,'" I said finally. "Don't get all dressed up in a tuxedo or anything."

They both looked at me as if I'd gone loony.

I tried to clarify. "Like with this basketball thing, Mom said I should just present my naked truth."

"Sarah, you *wouldn't!*" Christina cried.

"No!" I exclaimed. "That just means being honest."

"And taking the consequences?" Olivia asked.

I kind of slumped when she said that. "Yeah. Getting kicked off the team and missing the Pennsylvania game, and—"

"*Maybe* getting kicked off the team," Olivia corrected me.

"And *maybe* having kids tease you," Christina said to Olivia. "But maybe having them be nice, and getting to play soccer with us at recess because everyone will understand why you limp when you run."

It was Olivia's turn to sigh.

"And *maybe* getting a bad grade in Social Studies for refusing to do what the teacher tells you?" I asked Christina.

"*Definitely* getting a bad grade," said Christina. She hesitated. "But it'll be worth it." She grinned.

"Let's do it," I said. "Let's all three of us show our naked truth."

"We'll be the Three Naked Musketeers again," said Olivia.

"One for all!" Christina shouted, and held out her right hand.

"And all for one!" Olivia and I yelled at the same time, and we slapped our hands on top of Christina's.

"Look out, everybody," I cried. "This is who we are—*deal with it!*"

TEN

Olivia decided to go first, since she was tired of sweating in long pants anyway. She promised to wear shorts to school the next day, and we promised to beat up anybody who teased her or said anything bad about her.

I wasn't sure if she'd actually have the nerve to do it, but she did. She just showed up in the morning in a pair of khaki shorts and walked to her seat without once looking up.

Everybody stared. I wanted to tell them to mind their own business, but it must have been a big surprise, so I could understand them staring. Mr. Harrison came and gave our group, and especially Olivia, some extra attention on our

Language Arts work sheets. But other than that, he acted like everything was as normal as any other day.

When Olivia got up to sharpen her pencil, Jamal grabbed my arm in a panic. "What happened to her *leg?!?*" he whispered frantically.

I shook him off my arm. "She lost it in a car accident. Don't get hysterical."

"*Yesterday?!*" he squeaked.

"No, dummy," said Christina. "Two years ago. She just always wore long pants until today."

Jamal calmed down a little, and Olivia came back with her pencil. When it was almost time for lunch, we started discussing soccer.

"Tyrone's team has been winning way too much lately," said Jamal. "We've got to do something to turn that around."

"Yeah," I said. "We need new blood on our team. Olivia is going to play today."

Jamal's mouth hung open. "Oh, great," he said

sarcastically, "sure, that's a really good way to turn their winning streak around."

I kicked him hard under the desks.

"Ow!" He grabbed his ankle.

"I don't have to play," said Olivia angrily.

"No, you don't," said Christina. "And neither do we."

"I was in the mood to mess around on the jungle-gym today anyway," I said.

Jamal buried his head in his hands. "Okay, okay, you win," he said. "Can she run?"

"Who?" I demanded.

"What do you mean, *who?* Olivia. Can she run?" He bugged out his eyes in frustration.

"Why don't you ask *her?*" I said slowly. "She lost her leg, not her brain."

Jamal still didn't look Olivia in the eye. "Can you run?" he asked quietly.

"Yes," said Olivia. She held her head high.

"Can you kick?" he asked. "I mean, what can you do?"

"I played soccer a lot in Trinidad," she said. "I can kick, I can block, and don't worry, I know the rules. I'm not great or anything, but I can play."

The bell rang, and it was time for lunch. "See you at recess, Jamal," I said in a very sweet voice.

In the hall, the three of us girls slapped each other five.

"We've got power in numbers," said Christina.

"Thanks, you two," said Olivia.

All the way to the cafeteria, people stared. Even some of the teachers couldn't help staring at Olivia's artificial leg. But she just looked straight ahead and ignored them.

In the cafeteria, we walked right past the sixth-grade tables. Eric and Roger took one look at Olivia and started whispering to each other.

"Those guys say one mean word and they're dead," I said under my breath to Christina.

"Half a word," said Christina.

We stood in line for milk and then sat down

with our bag lunches. We chatted about soccer strategy, but I could tell Olivia was pretty uptight. As we gathered our trash, she said, "I'll stop in the girls' room before recess—check my strap and all for soccer."

"Go ask a lunch aide," I said. "They'll let you go now."

"We'll meet you at the soccer field," said Christina. "And we won't play without you, okay?"

Olivia agreed and left. As soon as she was gone, Eric and Roger came rushing over to us.

"Uh, we were wondering," Roger began.

"Yeah, we wanted to know . . . you know," Eric sputtered.

My memory flashed back to them in winter coats hogging the sledding hill, and Roger forcing Olivia into the concrete sewer drain.

"You wanted to know what?" I asked pleasantly.

"Did she—uh, did she get hurt?" Roger blurted out.

I elbowed Christina. "Yes," I said. "There was a sledding accident last winter."

"Yeah," Christina chimed in. "She somehow crashed into that sewer drain at the bottom of the hill."

Eric and Roger looked like they were about to pass out.

"I can't remember much," I said. "You know . . . the blood, the hospital . . . it was all kind of a blur."

"It's a shame," said Christina. "She's so young to have such a terrible thing happen."

Roger gripped Eric's arm and started to drag him away.

"Thanks for asking, guys," I called after them.

When they were out of sight, Christina and I collapsed with giggles. "I guess they won't be teasing Olivia," I said.

"They'll be too busy praying for our amnesia to last," said Christina.

Out on the soccer field, we met up with Olivia.

When it was time to start the game, Jamal called the three of us over with the rest of our team. He didn't fuss. He didn't roll his eyes. He just treated Olivia like any other new player. Two points for Jamal.

Olivia couldn't run nearly as fast as Christina or me, but boy, could she kick *hard!* She balanced on her good leg and swung her artificial leg from her knee. Since she didn't have to worry about hurting her foot, she could haul off and smack the ball with all her might.

The other team still played better than we did, and we still lost. But it was a lot of fun to play on a team with my two best friends. Olivia seemed like a very brave person to me that day. I hoped I could be as brave as she was when I went in to talk to the coach the next day.

ELEVEN

As I rode my bike to basketball practice, I planned what I would say to the coach. "Hey, Coach. What would you say if I told you you had a girl on your team?" Or how about "Have you ever thought of coaching a co-ed team instead of the boys' league? You've already had some experience, you know." Or my favorite so far, "My parents just found my birth certificate, and *guess what?*"

By the time I got to the church, I was sweating, from both the warm day and my nerves. I decided to test out the truth on Doug first, just to get some practice.

"Yo, Sam, wassup?" Doug tossed me a ball.

"Hey, Doug. You know what? My real name is Sarah."

Doug's face fell. "Wow. Bummer, man. What country are your parents from? Don't they know that in Maryland that's a *girl's* name?"

"Yeah," I assured him. "They named me Sarah *because* it's a girl's name."

Doug shook his head. "Sorry to hear that, dude. But that's okay. I'll just call you Sam, and I won't tell anybody."

He held out his hands for me to toss him the ball. I bounced it at him and went over to the sidelines to think of a better way to break the news to every-body. How about, "I have an announcement to make. I can't go to Pennsylvania with you all because it would be *illegal* for me to shower with the team." *No,* I thought. *I've got to be as direct as pos-sible.* I gritted my teeth, marched up to the coach, and tapped him on the shoulder.

"What do you need, Gajeski?" he said.

"Coach, I'm a girl."

"No, you're not," he said. "Don't be so hard on

yourself. In fact, you're one of the only players on this team who's *not* a girl. Now get out there and scrimmage."

I felt my eyes start to glaze over. Why couldn't I get anyone to believe me?

"Coach, listen to me." I pulled on his arm to make him face me. "I'm a *girl*, as in female. My name is Sarah Marie, not Sam. I didn't know this was the boys' league when I joined. I made a mistake. I'm a girl. Female. Understand?"

He blinked slowly. "You mean . . . you're a *girl?*"

Didn't I just say that? "Yes," I said.

He kind of stumbled over to a chair on the sidelines, and I followed him. "But . . . you're one of my best players." He sounded dazed.

I shrugged. "It can happen."

"And . . . I was counting on you—on Sam—for the game against the Tigers in Pennsylvania."

Here it comes, I thought. "Could we keep it a secret?" I begged. I knew it was last-ditch, but I had to try. "You could drop me off at the Holiday Inn— my mom isn't too keen on me sleeping in a bunkhouse or showering with a bunch of boys— and pick me up in time for the game. The other team would never know."

I was immediately sorry I'd made the suggestion. Coach scowled at me. "Right. And we'd get kicked out of the league for lying. This is a *church* team, Gajeski." He stood up. "We'll just have to make do without you."

I shoved my hands into my pockets and blinked back tears. "I really wanted to go," I said.

"Yeah," he said more gently. "I wanted you to go, too."

He marched onto the court to yell at my ex-teammates, and I walked slowly to the door of the gym. There, I turned and took one last look at the guys scrimmaging and the coach shouting orders. It sure had been a great bunch of games and a great team. Olivia had gotten to *start* playing soccer when she'd shown her truth. All I got was kicked off my team.

At home, Jerod was at the kitchen table snacking on peanut butter and bananas. I must have had a black rain cloud hovering above my head, because the second I walked in, he asked me what was wrong.

"I don't know about this 'come as you are' stuff," I said. "I'm thinking maybe 'fake everybody out' might be a better idea."

I told him what had happened with the coach, and he offered me a banana and a knife for the peanut butter. "Maybe next year you can join the girls' league," he suggested.

I stabbed the knife into the peanut-butter jar. "Do you have any idea how *far away* next year is?" I demanded.

"Yeah. I see your point," he said glumly. Then he brightened. "Hey, Sarah, you want my maroon-and-white sweater?"

Boy, I must really look pitiful, I thought. "But that's your favorite sweater. Why are you giving it away?" I asked.

He reached into his backpack. "It doesn't exactly fit me anymore." He pulled out what used to be his best wool sweater, the one he'd picked to wear to Sheila's party. It now looked like it might fit a Barbie doll. "Sheila put it in the dryer," he said.

I held the sweater up. "Bummer. Maybe we could wet it and stretch it."

He nodded. "Then it might fit *you.*"

I balled up the hopeless sweater so Jerod wouldn't have to look at it. "I'll see what I can do." On my way upstairs, I paused and said, "Hey, thanks for trying to help me feel better."

"No problem," he said.

As brothers go, Jerod is definitely one of the best.

TWELVE

Olivia and Christina both gave me hugs when I told them about getting kicked off the team.

"We can do something really fun the weekend of the Pennsylvania game," Christina offered. "Maybe my dad can take us to Kings Dominion—they've got a new roller coaster and everything."

"And maybe we can go camping again," said Olivia.

Having Christina and Olivia feel sorry for me cheered me up a little. And thinking about doing something fun with them helped, too. But I was still really disappointed.

Fortunately, Christina's pageant was coming up on Friday, so there wasn't a whole lot of time for me to sit around being miserable. We had plans to make.

When Christina had told her aunt about the pageant and Mrs. Green's Mexican costume, her aunt had gone into her closet and pulled out a great colorful dress and shawl that she'd worn in the town festival in Acajutla, El Salvador, when she was eleven years old. Christina was all excited, even though the outfit smelled like mothballs, and she told Mrs. Green about it. But instead of letting Christina switch, Mrs. Green said she'd already had the programs printed up, and she was sorry but they'd have to go ahead with Mexico, anyway, or the audience would get confused.

"I think she's in love with that dress she bought in Mexico," said Christina.

"Well, too bad for her," said Olivia.

We all giggled. We had plans for Mrs. Green's dress and her pageant, and it would all be a big surprise for her.

Christina had had to write a speech on Mexico, about the pyramids and the silver mines. It was pretty interesting, but she wrote an even better one on El Salvador, about its active volcano, Izalco, and the coffee plantations.

We put the new speech with the Salvadoran clothes in a white plastic bag. On the night of the pageant, Christina would act like she was going along with what she was supposed to do. She would dress up in Mrs. Green's outfit from Mexico, which she said was very itchy, and have the Mexico speech in her hands like she was ready to present it. Olivia and I would get seats with the rest of the audience and bring the white plastic bag. We would read the printed program, so we'd know when it would be Christina's turn. Two speeches before Christina's, Olivia and I would sneak backstage, get the bag to Christina, and help her change into the right clothes. She'd go out onstage with her aunt's dress and shawl and her El Salvador speech, and it would be too late for Mrs. Green to stop her. We congratulated ourselves for coming up with such a brilliant plan and waited for Friday.

Friday afternoon, I took a shower and washed my hair. It was growing out pretty well, so instead of putting on my baseball cap, I clipped a shiny blue-and-red barrette into it. Then I actually put on a blue skirt, a white blouse, and white dress shoes. There was no way anyone would mistake me for a boy at this pageant.

Olivia got dressed up, too, with a skirt that came below her knees so you couldn't see the little white sock and strap where her artificial leg was attached. The fake leg looked so much like her real leg I could hardly tell the difference. We walked together to the school, me with the white plastic bag under my arm.

The cafeteria had all the lunch tables pushed out of the way and metal folding chairs set on the floor in rows. Dressed-up parents held little kids by the hand, and two fifth graders from Mrs. Green's class gave out programs as we came in. Olivia and I said hello to Christina's parents, Mr. and Mrs. Perez, and her big brother, Antonio. Then we found seats in the front row and studied the program. Just before Christina was Jamal, and before him was Nailya, who was giving a speech on Russia.

"When Nailya starts, that's when we sneak backstage," I whispered to Olivia.

"Good," she said.

That would give Christina just enough time to change clothes, with me and Olivia holding up the Mexican poncho as a screen, and then step out onstage before Mrs. Green could see what was happening.

While Mrs. Green welcomed everyone and introduced the pageant, I got so nervous I wrapped the end of the plastic bag around and around my fingers until they looked like little red balloons. As the first few kids came out in their costumes to give their speeches, I tapped on my metal chair with my fingernails until the lady in front of me turned around and glared at me. Before Nailya was Tony, who was doing a speech on Maryland—stuff about the Chesapeake Bay and crabs. As soon as he finished, I nudged Olivia, and she got right up. I think she must have been pretty nervous and impatient, too.

We slipped quietly out the side door of the cafeteria and around the corner to the stage door.

"Okay," I whispered, trying to calm down. "We can do this, right?"

"Right," said Olivia. She let out a shaky breath.

We turned the handle on the stage door silently and pulled. Inside, it was dark. We saw a group of kids waiting in the wings, watching Nailya from side stage. Christina looked up from the group, saw us, and started over. What a relief! In a moment, we'd have her outfit changed, and in plenty of time for her grand entrance.

But before Christina got to us, like Frankenstein coming out of a closet, Mrs. Green stepped from the shadows and grabbed my shoulder. I almost screamed.

"What do you think you're doing backstage?" she demanded. "You're not part of this group."

"Uh . . . I think . . . we were . . ." I stammered.

"I don't care what you *think* you were doing," Mrs. Green hissed in a whisper. "I want you to leave the stage area this instant."

Christina groaned out loud. Our plan was crumbling. Onstage, Jamal, in his overalls and straw hat, had just started talking about tobacco farming in North Carolina. Mrs. Green impatiently shoved me toward the door.

Then, from the darkness next to me, I heard *zip-zip . . . crackle-crackle*. I knew that was the sound of Olivia's Velcro strap being undone, her leg being adjusted, and the strap being fastened again.

"Olivia, what—" I began.

But before I could say more, Olivia tripped, gasped, grabbed my arm for support, and started moaning, "Oh, ouch, *ow!*"

In the dim light I could just barely see that her left foot was turned out crazily—almost backward. The sight of it made me queasy.

"Olivia, what happened?" I cried.

Mrs. Green shushed us angrily. "I said, get out of the stage area immediately!" she ordered.

"But she's hurt herself!" I insisted.

Mrs. Green took one look at Olivia's foot and sucked in her breath. "Oh, my dear, what have you done?" She crouched to help Olivia, who grabbed onto her for dear life, like she would never let go.

"Quickly!" Mrs. Green motioned to Tyrone, who was standing there gawking. "Help me carry her out into the hall, where there's some light."

Olivia jerked her chin at me, and I finally caught on. I rushed to Christina and we ran to a corner. We ripped open the white plastic bag. But before

Christina could yank her costume off, we heard Jamal say, "So they also grow soybeans and corn on their farm, and when I go to visit, I help. Thank you very much."

"Christina, you're on. Let's *go*." A kid with a clipboard hovered over us.

Christina looked at me sadly. "It's okay. You guys tried, you really did." She started toward the stage, still dressed in the Mexican outfit.

I don't know what got into me. I ran ahead and stopped her. "It's my turn," I said. I pushed past the kid with the clipboard and walked out onstage all by myself.

I blinked in the bright lights. The audience looked up at me expectantly. My heart pounded so loud I couldn't hear anything else. "Uh, my name is Sarah, and I'm, uh . . . from Maine. Yeah, that's right, I'm from Maine."

I glanced to the side stage area. The kid was staring at his clipboard and scratching his head.

Christina and Nailya were rummaging through the plastic bag.

"And in Maine," I continued, "we have . . . um . . . a lot of, well, we have a shopping mall called the Maine Mall, and it has lots of stores like a drugstore and a pizza place, and a sporting goods store, and a place where you can get ice cream and stuff like that."

People in the audience started whispering to each other. I know I wasn't giving the best speech in the world, but it wasn't like I'd had much time to work on it, either.

"In Maine, the farmers grow, um . . . potatoes and lobsters and stuff. And we have lots of . . . lakes! That's right. In fact, I have a T-shirt that says there are five thousand, seven hundred, and eighty-five lakes in Maine, and I figure that must be true because otherwise they wouldn't have let them make a T-shirt that says that."

Another glance to side stage told me Nailya was

holding the poncho for Christina to change behind. I had to keep going.

"We also have lots of . . . snow. Yeah, it snows a lot. In fact, you guys hardly have any snow here compared to Maine, and I thought that was really weird this winter. I was glad it finally snowed *once*. I mean, really, you call that winter?"

By now, there was a lot of murmuring in the audience. I looked over and saw Christina standing ready in her Salvadoran dress and grinning.

"Thank you very much," I said, and got the heck out of there.

I heard "Hi, I'm Christina and my family is from El Salvador" before a very angry Mrs. Green gave me a fast escort into the bright lights of the hall. Olivia was already out there with her leg turned back to its normal position.

"What is the meaning of this?!" Mrs. Green's face was as red as the stripes on the Mexican poncho.

I learned a long time ago not to talk back to

teachers, so I didn't say, "We were just helping Christina show her truth," or, "You were trying to make Christina lie, but we fixed it so she didn't have to," or even, "You wouldn't listen to Christina, so we had to take matters into our own hands." I don't think she actually wanted an answer, so I didn't say anything.

"I've got your names. Your parents will be hearing from me," she growled. Then she stomped back through the stage door.

Olivia and I looked at each other and laughed a little. We wiped sweat from our faces.

"Christina got changed, and she's onstage right now," I told Olivia.

She held up one hand for me to slap her five.

"Great distraction," I said. "How long did it take Mrs. Green to figure out you were faking it?"

Olivia shrugged. "I don't know. I think I had her confused for some time. And then I finally took the leg off and said I had to see if my stump was bruised. She just stared at me like I was the bionic woman."

"Cool," I said. "You want to go see if Christina is still giving her speech?"

We decided not to go in, for fear of making Mrs. Green even angrier, but we peeked in the cafeteria doors. There was Christina, still onstage in her Salvadoran outfit, with a big smile on her face, talking about the Lempa River.

"At least Mrs. Green didn't pull her offstage," I said.

Olivia nodded. "And at least if we're in trouble, we're in it together."

"Don't worry," I assured her. "We're *definitely* in trouble."

THIRTEEN

We got an entire week of detention. But at least I was in detention with my two best friends instead of by myself, like I was at the beginning of the year. Christina got a zero for the pageant project because, Mrs. Green said, she hadn't been able to follow directions. That was going to make it almost impossible for Christina to bring her Social Studies grade up to a B for the next report card. But her father and mother were proud of her for speaking about their country. They said she deserved an A in sticking up for herself. And her father said that grades from fifth grade don't count for getting into college, anyway.

Olivia saw a couple of sixth-grade girls imitating the way she limps when she runs. I could tell it really hurt her feelings, but she said it was worth the teasing to get to play soccer, and at least nobody from our class gave her a hard time.

A week before the Pennsylvania game, the coach called my mom. He said the coach of the other team didn't mind a girl playing, and I was allowed to go! I'll bet the other coach thought a girl on the team would make it easier for his team to win. Anyhow, they'd set it up so I could stay at the Pennsylvania coach's house, in his daughter's bedroom. I could hardly believe it.

When we met in the church parking lot to get the bus to Pennsylvania, the guys from my team acted really weird. They kind of stood back and watched me, whispering to each other. My dad waited with me for the bus to arrive, and when it pulled up, he hugged me good-bye because he had to get to work. Then I felt really alone.

We piled onto the bus. Nobody sat with me, but even through the back of my head I could feel them staring. The coach figured out what was going on. He stood at the front of the bus to yell at us.

"Okay, folks, this used to be a boys' team, now it's a co-ed team. Big deal, stop your whispering." He pointed at me. "Somebody sit with Sam." Doug and Luther both got up and slid into the seat next to me. "Good. Now start acting like normal kids."

The coach, sat down and the guys started talking to me, saying they were really surprised when they found out I was a girl, and that I sure was an awesome basketball player, especially for a girl, and stuff like that. By the time we crossed the state line into Pennsylvania, we were all singing like a bunch of lunatics, pumped up like we thought we were a professional team or something.

It sounded like the guys were going to have a really fun night, the way they were wrestling and fooling around, so I was disappointed that I had to go to the coach's boring house, where everybody went to bed at nine o'clock. I had to sleep in a sleeping bag next to the bed of the coach's four-year-old daughter, who made little bubbling noises through her nose all night.

The next day, I found out the guys had had a blast. They'd had pillow fights and snack-food fights, until finally our coach stood in the bunk room and made everybody lie perfectly still and quiet until they all fell asleep. That wasn't until after midnight, and, boy, did the guys look it. They had puffy eyes, and on the court during warmups they were all stumbling around. The bubbly noises had kept me up a little bit, but I think I still looked better than they did.

We didn't play very well. We lost 52–30. But the bus ride back home was almost as much fun as the trip up, and all the guys said they hoped I'd get bubble gum in my hair next year so I could be on the team again.

Sunday afternoon, Jerod was getting ready to go to the movies with Sheila. Apparently, even though she'd thrown up on him and ruined his favorite sweater, he still liked her. He was in his room combing his hair, and I decided to watch. I figured even though it would be a while before I went out on a date, it never hurts to start learning about these things early.

"Are you going to wear your favorite shirt, or do you think that's too risky?" I asked.

Jerod smirked at me. "She doesn't throw up *all* the time," he said. He turned his head from side to side to make sure his hair looked good from all angles.

"Are you guys going to hang at the mall before you come home?" I asked.

"Yeah. Mom's not picking us up until six." He tucked in his shirt, examined it in the mirror, then untucked it again.

"Are you going to *buy* her something?" I asked.

Jerod made a face at me. "Maybe. I don't know. What does it matter to you?"

I shrugged. "I'm just taking notes on dating. In four

years or so I'll be in Sheila's position, and I want to know what's expected."

Mom called from downstairs that it was time to go, and Jerod was out the door before I could ask him who was paying for the movie.

I had just settled in to watch a baseball game on TV with Dad when there was a knock at the door. It was Doug with a basketball.

"You want to play some one-on-one?" he asked.

"How'd you find out where I live?" I asked. His bike was lying on the front lawn.

"Coach had your address."

And here I'd thought the kids on the team would ditch me now that the season was over and they knew I was a girl. I was glad to see that Doug was still treating me like one of the guys.

I said we could either play in the driveway or ride bikes up to the school, where there was more running space around the baskets. Doug opted for the school.

It was one of those spring days when everything is

lime Jell-O green and birds are singing. A great day for one-on-one.

At the school, we laid our bikes in the grass, and Doug let me have the ball first.

"Just try and stop me," I challenged him.

I faked a shot from the left, dribbled under the basket, and hooked it in from the right. Doug took the ball out, but I stole it from him easily and shot again. It bounced off the rim. I got the rebound and swished it in.

At first I thought I must be playing really great, but then I noticed that it was Doug who was playing lousy.

"You feel okay?" I asked.

He gave me a surprised look. "Sure. I feel fine."

"Then why don't you play like you mean it?" I was getting a little annoyed with him.

He started moving faster and blocking my shots, and made his next three baskets.

"That's better," I said.

When he went up for a jump shot, I leaped to block it, and we collided.

"Sorry," said Doug.

I stared at him. Sorry? Since when does one basketball player apologize to another in the middle of a hot game of one-on-one? Doug was definitely acting weird. I bounced the ball to him. "Here. Try again," I said.

This time I blocked his shot without touching him, grabbed the ball, and made a lay-up. "Too bad," I said.

Doug dribbled to the right and missed a short hook. I got the rebound and took it out. I dribbled with my back to him, shifting back and forth as he tried to slap the ball away. At one point, he slapped and hit my arm instead of the ball.

"Oh. Excuse me," said Doug.

I whipped around and faced him straight on. "What *is* your problem?" I blurted out. "You're being so . . . *polite*. Cut it out, will you?"

He looked at me sheepishly. "Okay," he said.

For the rest of the game, he went back to playing lousy, and I gave up trying to get him to change. On our way back to my house, I didn't even speak to him, I was so annoyed.

At my house, Doug got off his bike and followed me to the front door. He was kind of squirming, jostling from one foot to another and clearing his throat as if he had something to say but was too embarrassed to say it. I guessed he had to go to the bathroom, so I was about to tell him he could come in when he said, "Sarah, can I ask you something?"

"Okay," I said.

His eyes were wide and nervous, and he fidgeted with the corner of his shirt. "Will you come to the movies with me next Saturday?"

My mouth dropped open so wide you could have fit the basketball in there. So much for Doug treating me like one of the guys. And so much for me waiting four years before I go on my first date.

ELISA CARBONE is a full-time writer and a part-time windsurfer, rock climber, and lindy hop dancer. She is the author of *Stealing Freedom*, an ALA Best Book for Young Adults, and *Starting School with an Enemy*, her first book about Sarah. Ms. Carbone lives and seeks adventure in Maryland and the mountains of West Virginia.